The History
of the
Steel Band

by Verna Wilkins and Michael La Rose
illustrated by Lynne Willey

Tamarind

Many thanks to the following people for their help:
Sterling Betancourt and Beatrice El-Okbi,
Karin Stark and Sterling's Angels,
Kyla Thorogood, Ruth Thomsett,
Trinidad and Tobago High Commission,
Vastiana Belfon, Anne Faundez,
Franco Chen, Tom O'Leary

Published by Tamarind Ltd, 2006
PO Box 52
Northwood
Middx HA6 1UN

Text © Verna Wilkins, Michael La Rose
Illustrations © Lynne Willey
Editor Simona Sideri

Every effort has been made to trace any copyright owners of the photos and music
in this product (book + cd) and people who appear in the photos and to reference
their sources. Where any permissions have proved unobtainable then the publishers
will be pleased to hear from the owners and will be glad to correct any inaccuracies
as they deem appropriate.
Contact: www.tamarindbooks.co.uk

ISBN 1 870516 74 5

Printed in Singapore

Contents

Today steel bands still parade 'pan around neck' at Carnival.
This is Nostalgia at Notting Hill Carnival, London 1998.

Introduction

Today, the steel band is at the centre of world music. The melodious tintinnabulation of sticks striking steel can be heard at many musical events around the world. The steel pan is used in soundtracks for major movies and world famous musical artists like 50 Cent and Jean Michel Jarre have used steel band music.

Steel bands play an important part in Carnival parades all over the world. There are also huge steel band festivals in countries as far apart as North Korea and Switzerland. The steel pan, the only musical instrument to have been invented in the 20th century, has captured the hearts of people everywhere.

Who invented the steel pan? How was it invented? No one is quite sure, but there are many different stories. There are many stories about *who* started the steel band, and *how* it started. But everyone agrees about *where* the steel band started. It was in Trinidad, in the Caribbean.

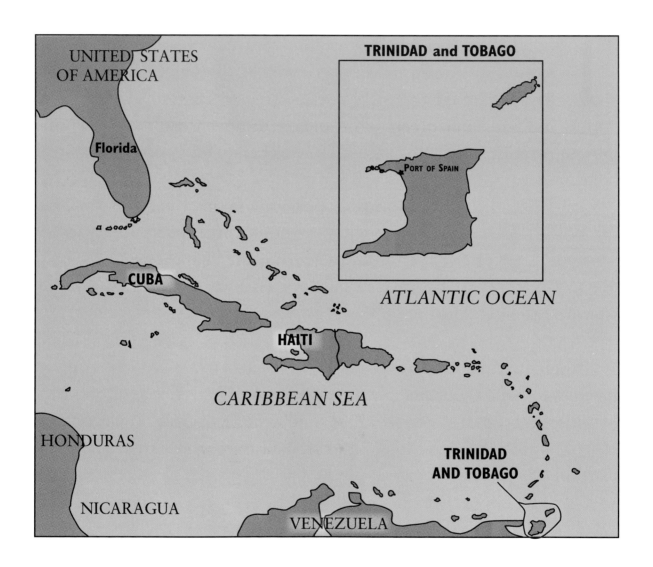

Map of Caribbean
with Trinidad and Tobago inset.

CHAPTER ONE

Treasure islands

The Caribbean islands are among the most beautiful islands in the world. They stretch from the southern coast of Florida in the United States, down to the northern coast of South America. These lush, green, tropical islands have white sandy beaches that stretch for miles along the blue sea. On the western coast of the islands is the Caribbean Sea. To the east is the vast Atlantic Ocean.

Trinidad and its smaller neighbour Tobago form the Republic of Trinidad and Tobago. Together, they measure 5128km^2 and have a population of about 1.3 million.

For hundreds of years, people who today we call Caribs and Arawaks, lived on the islands. They called the larger island, Cairi or Ieri. They had their own governments and leaders. They grew many sorts of crops and traded goods with other peoples who lived nearby.

Suddenly, their lives changed. On Tuesday 31 July, 1498, Christopher Columbus reached Ieri. The explorer was on a voyage around the world looking for new lands to conquer. He was working for King Ferdinand and Queen Isabella of Spain who wanted new lands and riches to add to their Spanish Empire.

Christopher Columbus re-named the larger island Trinidad (in Spanish meaning the Trinity, the name given by Christians to the three aspects of God) after three hills in the south of the island. He claimed the land for Spain. Today, its capital city is still called Port of Spain.

Columbus was sure that he would find gold on the island. He returned to Spain to tell King Ferdinand and Queen Isabella that he had discovered an 'El Dorado' (in Spanish meaning land of gold) where nuggets of gold, as large as goose eggs, could be found.

The islanders were left alone for a number of years, but in 1592, the Spanish returned. In their search for gold, they treated the local people brutally and forced them to work extremely hard.

The invaders soon realised that there was very little gold to be found on the island. But by then large numbers of native people had been worked to death. Many islanders also died from the diseases brought to the island by the foreigners.

The Spanish, however, were still keen to find some way of making money in the Caribbean. Since the climate of the islands was excellent for growing sugar cane, they began to harvest it and turn it into sugar. The sugar was then sold all over Europe.

Vast sugar plantations were started. But there were few local people to work on them since so many had died. So the Spanish travelled to Africa, where they captured and enslaved men, women and children. They brought them to Trinidad by force, made them work for no pay and took away their freedom.

The land was cleared and planted with sugar and cocoa. The plantations were owned by Spanish landlords and worked by enslaved people of African descent.

CHAPTER TWO

More arrivals

In 1793, the Spanish government decided to invite more people of European descent to settle in Trinidad. They proclaimed that they would give any Catholics who wished to go and live there 32 acres of land, for free. Many Spanish and French people left their homes and travelled to Trinidad to begin a new life. A great number

Workers cutting cane on a plantation.

Toussaint L'Ouverture,
a leader of the Haitian revolution

of the French people came from nearby islands, such as Haiti.

Years before they had taken over this large island to the north of Trinidad. They too had set up a harsh slave trade to provide themselves with free workers for their plantations.

After years of suffering brutality, the African workers in Haiti rebelled against the French and forced them to leave. Many went to Trinidad.

In 1797, the British arrived in the Caribbean. They, too, were looking for new territories to expand their empire. They fought and conquered the Spanish and claimed Trinidad as a British colony. They then brought their own enslaved workers from Africa to add to the population.

These workers were also made to work very hard. They, too, were brutally treated. After many years of suffering and exploitation, they began to fight for their freedom. They were joined in the struggle by many good people around the world, who realised that slavery was a most horrible injustice. At last, in 1834, the emancipation, or freedom, of slaves began.

Trinidadians of African descent were then free to leave the plantations. They moved to the towns and cities where they worked as tradesmen and labourers. This caused a serious labour shortage on the plantations so more workers were recruited, this time from Portugal and China.

These workers were not enslaved. They were brought to Trinidad as indentured

Harriet Tubman,
American abolitionist

labourers. This meant that they worked for no pay for five years and then were free to go home. But many of them stayed on the island after they were released. They too began to work for themselves and another labour shortage developed on the plantations.

Between 1845 and 1917, more than 140,000 Indians were brought to Trinidad, also as indentured labourers, to work on the plantations. The population continued to grow when migrants, looking for work, arrived from other Caribbean islands, especially from Grenada, Barbados and St Vincent.

Trinidad became home to many different peoples, who all kept their own cultural identities and musical traditions.

CHAPTER THREE

Musical culture

The original inhabitants of the islands, the Carib and Arawak peoples, had a musical culture of their own. Music and dance were an important part of life in the villages. They made drums from hollowed-out logs, and used gourds filled with pebbles to make a variety of different sounds.

The first inhabitants made music with hollowed-out log drums and gourds filled with pebbles.

Musical culture

The Africans who were brought to Trinidad also had a strong drum culture. They played drums during their many festivals and celebrations, and on special occasions, such as births, marriages and deaths.

They also used drums to send messages from one village to another. The rhythms and patterns of the drum beats had different meanings and could be heard over long distances. News could be spread quickly.

In Africa, drums were also used when people went to war, to scare the enemy and make their own soldiers feel brave.

In Trinidad, the rich plantation owners were not happy about the workers drumming. They knew that in Africa drums were used for communicating over long distances. They lived in fear that the workers would send messages between the plantations in order to organise themselves and rebel against the brutality and exploitation that they suffered.

At the same time, missionaries, who were mainly Roman Catholics, were trying hard to convert the workers to the Christian faith. They argued that it was anti-Christian to beat the drum.

Finally in 1883, in a desperate effort to get total control over the working people, the colonial government passed a law that banned drumming altogether.

African drums were made of wood and stretched animal skin.

CHAPTER FOUR

The origin of Carnival

Music and dancing were important to the workers of African descent. They held dances on Saturday and Sunday nights in their own homes and yards. They also celebrated Christmas and Easter with large parties. They created their own dances, such as the kalinda and the bamboula. Their

Trinidadians of African descent enjoyed parties with music and dancing.

The history of the steel band

instruments were their drums and chac-chacs (gourd rattles). They took turns to host weekend fêtes or parties.

The French had introduced Carnival to the islands. This was two days of serious partying just before Lent, a forty day period of fasting and repentance to remember the time Jesus spent in the wilderness.

The rich landowners celebrated Carnival by holding masked balls in their homes and in public halls, and there were parades on the streets of Port of Spain. The workers were not invited.

Artist's recreation of Carnival in Trinidad in the 19th century.

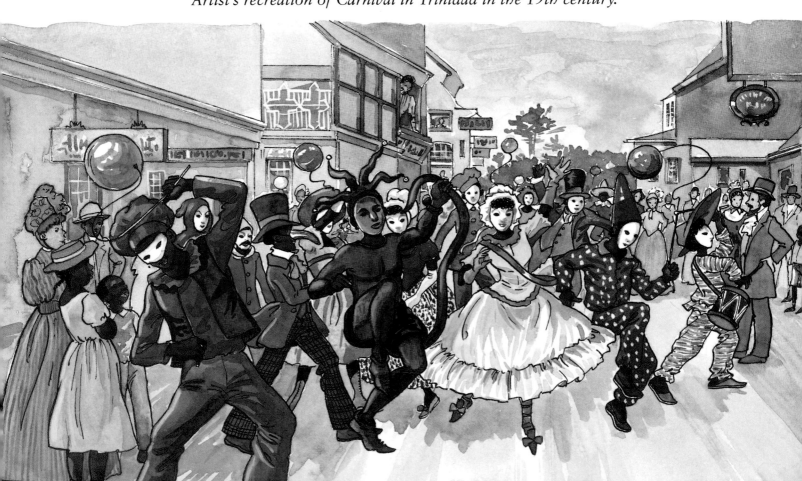

The origin of Carnival

Carnival was a time for mimicry, people dressed up in costumes and acted out important events. A favourite performance involved fighting a fire.

On the plantations, when a fire broke out at night in the sugar cane fields, gangs of workers were forced to go out and harvest the cane before it burned. They carried torches, while foremen blew horns and cracked whips at them. During Carnival, the plantation owners dressed up as African workers and took to the streets carrying torches, blowing horns and wearing masks.

The workers were not allowed off the plantations during Carnival, but they acted out the same fire fighting scene, with songs, dances and stick fights. They called this performance *cannes brûlées* (French for 'burnt canes'), which over time became 'Canboulay'.

After 1834, the workers took over the public carnival celebrations and brought with them the tradition of 'Canboulay'. But the colonial authorities were suspicious of it. They were afraid of the large numbers of people who took part in the parade and of the burning torches they carried through the streets of wooden houses.

Several attempts were made to keep down the number of people in the parade and to ban the drums. In 1881, the police tried to put an end to the merry-making. This led to the Canboulay Riots.

The police were not successful in ending the celebrations. Canboulay survived to become the Caribbean Carnival we know today and was to play a big part in the development of the steel band.

CHAPTER FIVE

Tamboo Bamboo

Drums of all shapes and sizes were banned in the 1930s by the colonial authorities. So Trinidadians of African descent were forced to look elsewhere for a musical instrument. They found inspiration in the bamboo plant.

Bamboo grew everywhere in the forest all over the island. People discovered that bamboo poles made a booming sound when struck with a stick or pounded on the ground. The larger the pole, the deeper the sound it made. To create a richer, more varied sound,

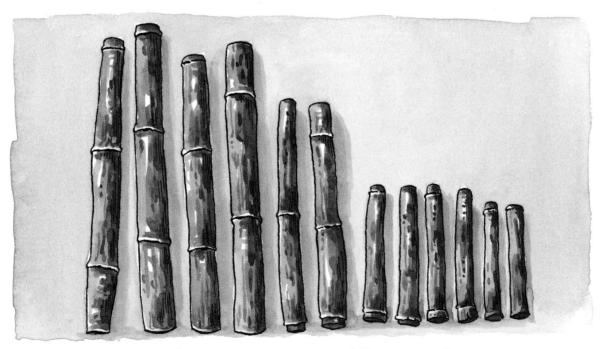

Bamboo cut to size to create different sounds.

the musicians hit bottles with pieces of metal or metal spoons to accompany the Tamboo Bamboo.

In Port of Spain, Tamboo Bamboo bands were started by unemployed young men in the poor neighbourhoods around Laventille, Gonzalez, East Dry River, Hell's Yard, Newtown and St James. There was fierce rivalry between these groups.

The pan maestro Sterling Betancourt, who was born in Trinidad in 1930, remembers his childhood. "We always had music. We had

Sterling Betancourt with Ellie Manette, another well-known pan maestro.

The history of the steel band

Tamboo Bamboo. When I was very young, even when my father was young, there were Tamboo Bamboo bands all over Trinidad. Bamboo was our musical instrument.

"I remember going with a group of young men, deep into the countryside, where the rainforests are, and where the green bamboo grew. We cut through the bamboo poles, tied them into bundles and took them home. We sorted them by size and then cut them into various lengths and left them to dry in the sun. We had to choose just the right time to harvest them. Otherwise, when dry, the poles would turn powdery and soft inside. We needed strong poles so that they could take a good pounding. Then we needed some smaller and thinner stems to make higher, lighter sounds. We made holes in the long stems. Depending on where we placed the holes, a different sound came out.

"We prepared loads of bamboo poles for the annual Carnival, which meant two days of serious merry-making with dancing in the street. Hundreds of dancers followed the Tamboo Bamboo bands from early morning till late at night."

A Tamboo Bamboo band ▶

Tamboo Bamboo

CHAPTER SIX

Beating pan

Many people have stories about their part in inventing the steel band. But who first thought of beating metal containers and tins to make music? There are various different stories...

Alfred Mayers, another pioneer of the steel band movement, claims that "beating pan" began because the musicians were left empty-handed when their bamboo smashed to pieces after hours of playing. During Carnival, they had to continue to bang out a rhythm to keep the dancers going for as long as possible. So they looked around for things that could make a noise and picked up any empty cans they found lying around.

Sterling Betancourt agrees with Alfred Mayers and adds, "the problem, especially with the big bass bamboo, is that after a heavy pounding on the road surface for many hours, it would split and fall apart. Some careless dancers even hurt themselves by accidentally smashing the bamboo pole onto their foot, or even someone else's! There were some serious accidents.

"The Tamboo Bamboo players then picked up tins and bottles, beating a rhythm to keep the show on the road. I believe they then discovered that some tins made better sounds than others. Eventually people in the bands began to look for better-sounding tins, and gradually the steel band evolved."

Beating pan

The musicians tried out all sorts of metal objects.

Carlton Forde, a famous calypso* singer of the time, tells how, around late 1935 or early 1936, a young man in his band found an empty paint can by the side of the road. When he hit it, the can made some good sounds.

Carlton and his friends then began to look for other cans that made those special sounds. They managed to collect a range of paint cans that produced various single musical notes. They practised beating

* Trinidadian musical style developed by African workers.

out rhythms until they could play some real tunes. But they found that, although the notes were quite clear, these 'found' instruments had a terribly tinny sound.

They needed deeper, richer sounds. So they experimented with cans of different sizes. Eventually, they found a large metal biscuit tin that produced a good deep sound. This was used for the bass.

Another great name in the history of the steel band is Winston 'Spree' Simon. He lived in John John, a poor area of Port of Spain. Here 'Spree' got involved in music and soon became one of the best players in the John John Steel band.

Near John John was a railway repair yard. It was a good place to find old cans and other metal objects that could be used as instruments. The range of sounds the cans produced when struck with different objects caught 'Spree' Simon's attention.

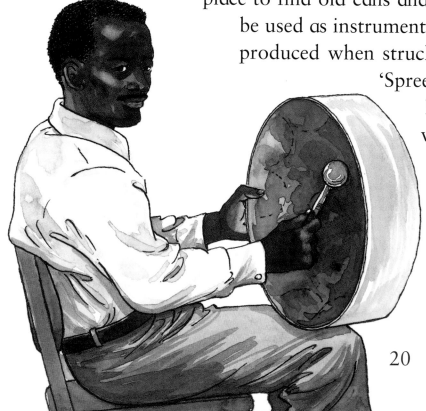

He then began to experiment with sound. He says, "One evening, the John John Band was parading in the village. I wanted a rest from drumming so I lent my kettledrum to a friend, Wilson Bartholomew, alias Shaker. When I returned to

◀ *'Spree' Simon*

20

collect it, I noticed that the face of the pan was beaten in very badly and the particular tone, or sound, was gone. I also noticed its concave appearance.

"Using a stone, I started pounding the inside of the drum to restore it to its original shape. While pounding, I discovered that the metal had different strengths. I was amazed. I was able to get different notes.

"Then I tried using a piece of wood. The sounds were a little warmer. I was fascinated. I was able to get clear and separate musical notes. I turned my knowledge over to the other members of the John John Band, and pan was born."

What matters is that pan was invented, not *who* invented it. As Sterling Betancourt points out, "Some say that no one person invented pan. That might well be so. But whatever happened, it was wonderful, and now pan has spread all over the world from where it was invented, in my home, in Trinidad."

CHAPTER SEVEN

All-steel bands

So, alongside the Tamboo Bamboo band, a new musical sound started to evolve, created by the rhythmic beating of various metal objects. All types of metal objects and containers were being tried out. These included empty paint tins, large Bermudez biscuit tins, car hubcaps and even dustbin lids.

The metal instruments did not break or split, or inflict the injuries caused by the splintering bamboo, so they became more popular. They also made stronger and more varied sounds. Steel and iron percussion instruments began to replace bamboo in the Carnival. While some of the older band members continued to play the bamboo, the younger men experimented. After some initial resistance, everyone began to accept the change.

Each band wanted to be the best and they chose interesting names for themselves, such as the Invaders, Desperadoes, Highlanders and the Red Army Band, among others. Then there were the bands with names taken from American movies – Casablanca, Destination Tokyo and Renegades.

The musicians worked hard to make richer, smoother sounds and there was fierce competition. So much so, that a large number of bands, each representing a specific district, have laid claim to being the first to produce a 'real' note on the steel pan.

The newspapers of the time all agreed that it was in and around

To begin with, musicians played bamboo as well as the new steel instruments.

Port of Spain that the fastest and most important changes from bamboo to steel occurred. It was in Newtown, at Carnival of 1937, that the first all-steel band paraded through the streets without any bamboo at all. They used the steel pans to create both the rhythm and the melody of their music.

Carlton Forde led the band, wearing a costume of top hat and tails. Alfred Mayers, a commentator at the time, reports, "They were well dressed. There was a bandmaster, like a conductor. He had a black long-tailed coat, top hat and stick. You should have

23

At Carnival, the steel bands paraded in interesting and colourful costumes.

seen him conducting the band! He caused quite a stir in town, man. Others had on jackets and bow ties. The band was all metal. A lot of people followed them. They were so popular."

Steel bands began to dominate Carnival. They provided most of the music for the celebrations and accompanied the calypso singers.

CHAPTER EIGHT

Banned!

The pan players, who were mostly young men from poor areas, had an interesting but violent reputation. Some were known as 'Bajorns' (bad Johns) for their fierce street-fighting habits. Others named themselves 'Saga Boys' (stylish playboys). There was rivalry among them, and they often clashed on the streets.

The British colonial authorities opposed these newly formed musical bands. They wanted to end their influence among the unemployed urban youth. The police took advantage of the regular fights and 'band clashes' to arrest the players and destroy their pans.

Newspapers printed articles criticizing the players, and church leaders preached against them. Many ordinary people also opposed the steel band culture. Families stopped their children playing in the bands or getting involved in any way with the new musical culture. It was very difficult to be a pan player in the face of this opposition.

Sterling Betancourt was a lucky exception. When his mother found out he was playing pan, she was angry and disappointed, but she supported his choice.

It was when he was about 13. His mother wanted Sterling to do well in his exams and had arranged private lessons for him after school. One afternoon, when he was supposed to be attending a lesson, he had instead gone to join some friends who were making music and tuning pans.

The history of the steel band

Sterling's friends saw his mother coming towards them and warned him. He began to run away.

But his mother called out, "I've seen you Sterling. Don't bother to run!" Sterling turned and walked towards her with his head down, expecting the worst.

Instead, she said, "Is that what I am paying my hard earned money for? Here you are, under a tree, tuning pan! But okay, if that is what you want, you can have it. No more expensive private lessons then. I'll buy you a steel drum. You can do that instead."

From then on she supported her son's choice and took no notice of anything family and friends said against it. Most other parents would have banned their children from ever playing pan again.

During World War II, Carnival was banned in Trinidad by the colonial authorities. Despite this, the development of the steel pan as a musical instrument went on at a feverish pace in the poorer parts of Port of Spain.

When victory in Europe was announced in 1945, crowds spilled onto the streets of Port of Spain in an unplanned VE Day Carnival. Steel bands provided the music for this celebration which helped them begin to gain respect and acceptance in Trinidad.

But it was not until 1951 and the TASPO – Trinidad All-Steel Percussion Orchestra – tour of Britain that the steel band began to be recognized and appreciated by the authorities in Trinidad.

Lieutenant N. Joseph Griffiths conducting The Trinidad All-Steel Percussion Orchestra at Alexandra Palace, London on the 24th August 1951 as part of the programme 'Caribbean Cabaret'.

TASPO was formed to represent Trinidad at the 1951 Festival of Britain, an exposition of arts, crafts and culture from all around Britain and its colonies. Sterling Betancourt, Ellie Manette and 'Spree' Simon were all among the musicians in this band.

CHAPTER NINE

Pounding the pan

During World War II Trinidad supplied Britain with oil from its oilfields in the San Fernando valley, and the USA had a naval base in Trinidad. For this reason, there were many empty 55-gallon oil drums lying about. Musicians noticed and started to use them to make their pans.

The oil drums were made from better steel than the Bermudez biscuit tins that players had been using, and they produced notes of a much higher musical quality.

These large 55-gallon drums are often still used today. It is a complicated procedure to turn them into musical instruments.

Cutting the 'skirt'.

To make a steel pan, the 55-gallon steel oil drum is cut through from side to side. The side of the drum is called the skirt. The length of the skirt affects the sound it produces and determines the 'voice' of the pan.

A short skirt gives a high-pitched sound and a long skirt makes a low-pitched sound.

Pounding the pan

'Sinking' the drum.

The next stage is 'sinking' the drum. A sledgehammer is used to pound the top of the drum into a concave (bowl) shape. The pounding stretches the steel and prepares the surface. This is the hardest and noisiest part of the job. It can take up to 5 hours to hammer a pan into shape!

The pan maker marks the pan to show where the notes will go.

The bowl of the pan is then marked up with all the different notes. The outline of each note has to be carefully drawn on the metal. Sometimes templates are used to show where each note will go. Marking up the pan is quite a tricky job, but it is very important if the next stage – which is the 'grooving' of the notes – is to go smoothly.

29

'Grooving' the pan to separate the notes.

The outline of each note must be punch-marked all the way round with rows of tiny holes. This 'grooving' is done with a nail punch and a hammer. It marks the notes out clearly so they are easy to see when the pan is played. It also separates the notes and stops the vibration of one note interfering with the notes beside it making sure the sound of the instrument is clear and clean.

Then comes the difficult part. Using a mallet the spaces between the notes are raised into convex shapes or bumps to form the notes themselves. All of this hammering must not break the metal and must not stretch it too much in one place compared to another.

Finally, the marked out surface is placed in a hot furnace. This hardens the steel, making the notes hold their sound.

Pounding the pan

Then the pan is 'coarse tuned'. Pan tuners are highly skilled people who, like piano tuners, use their ears and electronic devices to get the correct pitch for each note. They work with a hammer and a rubber-tipped tuning stick. This is when the notes are tuned to exactly the right pitch before the instrument can be passed for playing.

The tuned steel pan has to be protected from rust, so a layer of zinc or chromium is applied to the surface. This gives the pan an attractive bright silver finish, but it can alter the tuning so the pan tuner has to hammer the notes again, back to perfect pitch.

The steel pan is played with two sticks, one in each hand. The sticks vary in length and are tipped with rubber strips or sponge balls depending on what the player prefers and which pan they are playing.

The steel pan was originally slung around the player's neck and rested at waist level. It is still sometimes played that way today when a steel band parades on foot. At the head of every steel band is a dancer heralding the procession through the streets with an intricate dance and waving a flag. This is the celebrated 'flag woman' or 'flag man'.

CHAPTER TEN

Development of steel bands and Panorama

In the first steel bands, the musical range was limited. The high notes were produced on pans called 'Ping Pong'. 'Strummers' produced the mid-range notes, and the bass pan was called the 'Dudup' or 'Doo Dup', which reflects the sound it makes. The percussion instruments or 'iron section' (scrapped brake drums of

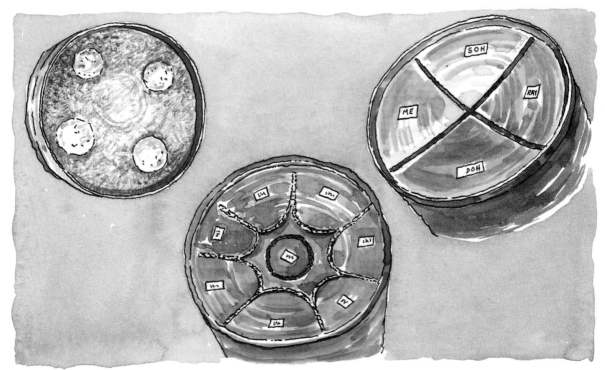

Some early steel pans

cars and trucks, played with metal rods) carried the rhythm. This made the distinctive sound of the steel band.

As techniques advanced, steel bands grew into steel orchestras, where each pan or group of pans contained all the notes in the musical scale. This is the same musical range as a classical orchestra and gave the steel band the possibility of playing a much wider range of music.

As the bands in Trinidad grew both in importance and musical ability, regular competitions called Steel Band Music Festivals started, where both calypso and classical music were played. These festivals were highly competitive with each band and each soloist trying to be the best. One famous soloist of the 1950s was Dudley Smith, who played Beethoven's *Minuet in G* to win the Solo Ping Pong competition.

Today, the most important competition for the steel bands in Trinidad and Tobago is the Panorama. Established in 1965, this is an annual national competition held during the carnival celebrations. There are preliminaries, semi-finals and finals. The final takes place on the Savannah racecourse in Port of Spain and is attended by thousands of steel band fans.

Each steel orchestra has a captain, a tuner, an arranger (who adapts a piece of music so it can be performed by the pans and players in that particular orchestra) and as many as one hundred players. The bands play complicated pieces that include classical music, calypso, salsa, pop, reggae and soul, along with music especially composed for the steel band.

Each band chooses a tune for the Panorama, usually a calypso. The selected tune, which must last 8 to 10 minutes, is arranged in a way that will show off all the band's skills. The winner is proclaimed Panorama Champion.

Between 1960 and 1980, many excellent arrangers emerged. Among them were Ray Holman, Clive Bradley, Robert Greenidge, Rudy Smith, Jit Samaroo and Len 'Boogsie' Sharpe, who competed fiercely for musical supremacy. These musicians no longer just arranged calypso tunes for their bands, but composed (wrote) their own, new music for the steel orchestras. These were beautiful and complex pieces.

Most pan players play by 'ear'. They do not read music. They learn the music through punishing repetitive drills and practice. These complicated arrangements are performed with lightning flashes of the wrists and choreographed movements of the players' arms and bodies.

Today, there are more than one hundred steel bands in Trinidad and Tobago, each with its own history. One of the most impressive aspects of the bands is their sheer size. Many are among the largest music groups in the world.

CHAPTER ELEVEN

From Trinidad to the world

The steel band spread first through the Caribbean islands, where there are now a large number of bands, and then it spread around the world. In recognition of this global steel band musical phenomenon, the first World Steel Band Music Festival was organised in Trinidad in 2000.

Steel band music is today used all over the world in education to bring better cultural understanding and appreciation of music. It is also used as music therapy to benefit both adults and children.

Sterling Betancourt recalls his role in exporting this enduring musical form to the world. "I helped to spread our steel band to many parts of the world. I travelled from Trinidad to England in 1951 with the Trinidad All-Steel Percussion Orchestra, TASPO. We took part in the Festival of Britain as the first steel band to play in Britain. We represented the best of all the steel bands in Trinidad.

"I now have a steel band group in Switzerland and in Germany, where I spend time every year. It gives me great pleasure to see and hear marvellous steel bands in schools and universities all over the world."

Today, there are steel bands in Britain and all across Europe, from France, Holland and Germany to Switzerland, Sweden and Denmark. There are bands across the whole of the USA and Canada, in schools,

The history of the steel band

universities and cities with Caribbean communities. Steel bands are even to be found in Japan.

The sound of the pan has come to be recognised as the sound of Trinidad and the Caribbean. It is born of the creativity, invention and musical genius of unemployed urban youth from deprived communities. It is testimony to the power of the steel band that the music has survived its small beginnings and has spread throughout the world.

◀ *Steel bands sometimes parade on trucks at the Notting Hill Carnival.*

Sterling Betancourt and Sterling's Angels steel band

Sterling Betancourt was born in Trinidad in 1930. He began playing music when he was still a child, joining a Tamboo Bamboo band in his hometown of Port of Spain.

He moved on to the steel pan and soon became an expert. In 1951 he was chosen to represent Trinidad at the Festival of Britain with the Trinidad All-Steel Percussion Orchestra (TASPO).

After touring for six months with TASPO, Sterling decided to settle in the UK. He worked teaching children and adults how to play this new instrument.

In 1963 Sterling and a group of other pan men took part in the Children's Carnival. They took a walk down the street, pan-around-neck, and more and more people joined in and followed the band. Out of this small parade, developed the Notting Hill Carnival, which today is Europe's biggest street carnival attracting over 2 million visitors.

In 2002, Sterling received an M.B.E. (Member of the Order of the British Empire). He is the first steel band pioneer to be honoured and recognised for his services to steel band music. In 2003 he was made a Fellow of the Royal Society of Arts.

Sterling Betancourt and Sterling's Angels steel band

Sterling and friends in 1963.

The history of the steel band

In 1967 Sterling travelled to Switzerland to perform. He has returned there many times over the years to teach and inspire players, and to form the first Swiss steel band. He taught many Swiss children to play pan.

In November 1999 some of these children decided to start their own steel band, calling themselves Sterling's Angels.

There are six young players in Sterling's Angels steel band, who rehearse once a week at their 'pan yard'. Whenever Sterling visits he teaches them new tunes so they now have a repertoire of about 50 pieces arranged by Sterling in the traditional calypso style.

In 2004 they produced a CD, *Live nice!* They have kindly given us permission to reproduce a selection of their songs in order to illustrate the range of music and sounds a steel band can create.

Photo credits

Cover: Ellie Mannette (detail of pic from p.15), see below for credits
Title page: Sterling Betancourt, Notting Hill Carnival 1997 © Franco Chen
Opposite p.1: Sterling Betancourt and Nostalgia, Notting Hill Carnival 1998 © Franco Chen
page 15: Sterling Betancourt and Ellie Manette 2002 © Annette Hudemann
page 27: Picture shows Lieutenant N. Joseph Griffiths conducting The Trinidad All-Steel Percussion Orchestra at Alexandra Palace on the 24th August 1951 as part of the programme 'Caribbean Cabaret'. Players are Theo 'Black James' Stephens, Belgrave Bonaparte, Andrew 'Pan' de la Bastide, Philmore 'Boots' Davidson, Orman 'Patsy' Haynes, Winston 'Spree' Simon, Dudley Smith, Ellie Mannette, Sterling Betancourt, Granville Sealey, Anthony Williams. Copyright © BBC.
page 36: Children's Day of the Notting Hill Carnival in London 28th August, 1999. Picture by: PA. © EMPICS.
page 39: West Hampstead Children's Carnival 1963. At the front, Sterling Betancourt, Miguel Baradas, Russel Henderson with his head turned, behind them are Ed Paterson and Ralph Cherrie. © unknown, reproduced with permission from Sterling Betancourt.
Back cover: Sterling Betancourt (detail of pics from p.39 and p.15)

Sterlings' Angels
Live nice! CD (selection)

1. Footprints in the sand – trad.
2. Politician – Sterling Betancourt
3. Sankee soca – Sterling Betancourt
4. Blueberry Hill* – trad.
5. Guantanamera – trad.
6. Jamaica farewell, Island in the sun* – trad.

Recorded at Eliza's Home, Hohentannen, Switzerland, July 2004
Recording and mix: Yves Maino
Special thanks to Eliza Pfäffin
A real steel production by Yves Maino

Musicians:
Janine Bichsel and Karin Stark – tenor pan
Doris Stark – second pan
Sabrina Bichsel and Ramona Stark – guitar pan
Roman Röthlisberger – bass-pan*
Sterling Betancourt – bass-pan, percussion